REM▲DE

A SERIAL IN 15 EPISODES

BY

MATTHEW CODY

KIERSTEN WHITE

E.C. MYERS

ANDREA PHILLIPS

CARRIE HARRIS

GWENDA BOND

SERIAL
BOX

serialbox.com

For additional information and permission requests, write to the publisher at Serial Box Publishing 175 Varick St. 4th Fl, New York, NY, 10014.

ISBN: 978-1-68210-094-3

Written by: Matthew Cody
Cover Design: Elizabeth Casal
Lead Writer: Matthew Cody
Editor: Noa Wheeler
Producers: Julian Yap & Molly Barton

REM▲DE

SEASON **01** · EPISODE **01**

SHADOWS AND DREAMS

BY

MATTHEW CODY

SERIAL
BOX

ReMade
Season 1, Episode 1

Shadows and Dreams
Matthew Cody

Someone shouted Holden's name. A girl's voice, calling to him—or had he been dreaming? Either way, he didn't like getting yelled at. He wanted to ask her to calm down, he wanted to ask what was wrong, but when he tried to talk his tongue stuck to the roof of his mouth like cotton. He opened his eyes, but the bright light overhead burned spots into his vision. He closed them again and he saw little exploding stars.

"I'm sorry," he mumbled, but his words didn't sound right in his own ears. His thick tongue got in the way.

Then the dream—surely he must be dreaming—changed. A beautiful girl leaned over him. Almond skin and a dusting of glitter on her cheeks like frost. She wore a crown of leaves in her hair.

She whispered in his ear. "O, how I love thee. How I dote on thee!"

Holden knew that face. It belonged to Titania the Fairy Queen. Wait, that wasn't right.

The Fairy Queen suddenly screamed his name, terrified.

The next time he opened his eyes there were monsters. They surrounded him, poked at him with spindly metallic arms. He saw himself reflected in their glassy eyes, multifaceted like prisms. A dozen Holdens all screamed at once, but someone had turned his voice off. There was no sound. When he tried to fight back his body wouldn't do what he asked it to. He couldn't even close his eyes anymore; he couldn't blink. He had to watch what they were doing as they jabbed him with needles that made his body spasm.

"He's awake," said a voice near his ear. Rough, gravelly. Not like Titania's at all. "You shouldn't do this to him while he's awake. It hurts him."

All at once the metal spiders froze, like Holden was

living in a video that had stopped playing. *Buffering . . . buffering . . .*

They came back to life as one of them jabbed another needle into Holden's throat.

"It hurts him!" said the voice again, and Holden was looking into the face of one of the ugliest women he'd ever seen. Her heavy brow and broad, whiskered chin made her look almost simian. But she smiled at him with her yellow, crooked teeth and laid a hand on his forehead.

"Go back to sleep," she whispered in his ear. "We'll wake you when it's all over." There was a tiny pinprick as she stuck him with a needle of her own, but this one didn't hurt so much. Within seconds all the pain went away and Holden was sinking into a warm, dark bath. The woman's hands were rough and calloused, but she was gentle as she brushed her fingers over his eyes, closing them for him as one would for a corpse.

Two things occurred to him before he slipped back into darkness. First, he wondered if Titania would be waiting for him. And second, he feared that he hadn't been dreaming at all.

• • •

Holden Black wanted to be absolutely sure he'd be the last one out of the building, so he sat alone in his dressing room and waited. It was really a storage closet, but for the weekend run of *A Midsummer Night's Dream* it did double duty. For the time being, he had to share it with a plastic mop bucket on wheels and several crates of industrial-strength cleaner—the kind that was strong enough to dissolve dried gum off desks. Using grease paint from his makeup kit, Holden had drawn a smiley face on one of the bottles and started using it as a wig stand. Unfortunately, the school janitors still used this closet during the daytime, because when Holden arrived at half-hour tonight there was a note taped to it that read, "Pls clean! NOT a toy!"

Holden's sparkly wig now hung on a mop pole instead.

Being the only male, Holden couldn't dress with the other fairies, so he was stuck with a makeshift dressing room inside a janitor's closet. That meant he was also closest to the "cafetorium" that doubled as a stage. Laughter and congratulations filled the lobby just outside his door. The closet didn't lock from the inside, so Holden changed into his street clothes as fast as he could, making sure to keep his back to the door. Not that anyone would get curious about a janitor's closet, but still. Holden could just picture that door accidentally opening onto a crowded roomful of teenagers and their parents, and him standing there in his boxer briefs and eye shadow. It would be a Holden moment to remember.

He nearly tripped over his own legs as he yanked his jeans on, but it was even harder getting off his glittery stage makeup. The only water in the closet came out of a slop sink, and Holden didn't trust the brownish liquid that sputtered from that faucet, so he did the best he could with wet wipes and a handheld mirror. The glitter had gotten everywhere, and the eye shadow made him look like a raccoon. His fairy tights had given him jock itch.

I should take a picture of all this crap, he thought. *Start a Tumblr called "What's the stupidest thing you've done for love?"*

He finished cleaning off his makeup as best he could, but there were still voices outside. People sure were taking their time high-fiving one another.

To pass the minutes, Holden used the grease paint to doodle on a few more bottles of cleaner. At first he kept the smiley face theme, but then he switched to really pissed-off faces. After all, how would you feel if you were a bottle of industrial strength gum dissolver? He hid these ones way in the back of the crates. Maybe one day they'd give someone a laugh.

He ignored the lone card on his makeshift dressing table. It sat there unopened, with his name written in curling letters and the message "Break a leg!" carefully hand drawn to look like the words were exploding out of a champagne bottle. Holden hadn't read what was on the inside. Eventually he would, just not yet.

In time, the commotion outside his door died down and Holden grabbed his backpack. Three new texts on his phone, all from the same person, but he didn't read them. Time for that later. He started out the door, stopped, went back for the unopened card, and shoved it into his pocket.

I'll deal with it tonight. I will.

The cafetorium was finally empty. The rest of the cast would already be headed to the opening night party, but not Holden. No cast party, no way. He'd rather die than spend the next few hours glued to the snack table. *Don't mind me. I don't care if no one bothers to talk to me. I'm cool being alone. Just me and the onion dip, yo.*

He couldn't go home yet, anyway. There were still the unanswered texts on his phone, the unopened card in his backpack. His phone buzzed in his pocket. *Shit.* He couldn't put it off any longer. *I'll stop by on the way home. We'll talk. Make it quick, like pulling off a Band-Aid, right?*

Right. He should at least read the card first. It would be a dick move not to—he resolved to read it just as soon as he got to his car.

Holden thought he'd be the last one to leave, but when he stepped out into the parking lot he was surprised to find another car still there. By the light of the streetlamps he recognized the Darwin fish-with-legs sticker on the back bumper, incongruously sandwiched between stickers for Amnesty International and the Police Officers' Association.

Holden stopped and stared, his car keys dangling from his hand and his heart pounding up near his ears.

Seyah Jackson sat in the driver's seat, her face lit blue by the glow of the phone she held to her ear. She kept turning the key in the ignition, but nothing happened. Holden stood there like a dumb statue, like a bottle with a face painted on it. After a few more tries she finally gave up and opened the car door. That's when she spotted Holden standing there in the shadows.

"Wait, stay on with me for a minute," she said into the phone. "There's some guy standing here watching me."

Some guy?

Of course. He must look like a psycho killer standing stock-still in the dark parking lot. Christ, he was straight out of a Japanese horror film.

"Hey, Titania," he said, stepping into the light of the streetlamp. "It's me!"

She stopped and squinted at him. "Peaseblossom?"

"Uh, Mustardseed, actually," he said. "Something wrong with your car?"

She relaxed a little and talked into the phone. "No, it's one of the fairies. Mustardseed . . . Yeah, the boy one. Hold on." She cupped her hand over the phone and said to Holden, "It won't start."

Holden knew absolutely nothing about cars, so what he said next was pointless, but it seemed the thing for a guy to do. "You want me to take a look?"

"It's cool," she said, still talking into the phone. "Let me call you back." Then, smiling at Holden, "I think the battery's dead. I probably left my lights on."

"I do that all the time." He'd never done it even once.

"I'm sorry, but I'm totally blanking on your name."

"Oh, it's Holden. We ran lines together once on a break. Well, you ran lines, I didn't really have any in that scene." Or any at all. The director had cut Holden's part, which was small to begin with, down to a walk-on role.

"Right, of course. I didn't want to keep calling you Mustardseed."

"The name sucks," said Holden. "Titania's not bad, though. Shakespeare was better at naming his leads, I guess."

"I guess. So, do you want me to pop the hood?"

"Huh?"

"You said you could take a look at the engine."

"Oh, yeah," said Holden. "Yeah, pop the hood. I'll look at the engine and see if . . . You know. What's up in there."

Holden lifted the hood as Seyah leaned over his shoulder and used her phone as a flashlight. He tried to keep his eyes on the engine and not stare directly at her from only inches away. Because that would be creepy. Almost as creepy as commenting on how good her shampoo smelled, not too flowery but tart like a freshly sliced lemon.

That would be *super* creepy.

"Hmm." Holden touched a few things under the hood. Tapped on a metal thing here, peered interestedly at that other thing there. "I don't really see anything wrong." It was technically true.

Seyah sighed. "Yeah, I think it's the battery. My friends were gonna leave the cast party and come and get me, but you don't have any jumper cables, do you?"

Holden paused as he pictured the cables his dad made him carry in his trunk. They were still wrapped in the store plastic, ready to use.

The phone vibrated in his pocket. Another text. And a split-second decision.

Yeah, what is the stupidest thing you've ever done for love?

"No jumper cables, sorry," lied Holden. "But if you want, I can give you a ride to the party. I'm headed there anyway."

• • •

Holden mumbled lame excuses and apologies as he cleared the McDonald's wrappers and Starbucks cups off the passenger's seat. As Seyah got in, she sniffed. "Still got that new car smell."

Holden took a whiff. Stale coffee and day-old hamburger pickles. When he'd parked his car that morning he hadn't dreamed that he'd be cleaning the seat off for Titania herself, but here he was . . .

Blowing it. "Oh. Yeah, I'm sorry about the smell. I can run that stuff back inside to the trash if they haven't locked up yet."

"No," said Seyah, smiling. "It's fine. It was a joke. A shitty joke. You're giving me a ride and all."

Holden nodded, relieved. "I'll crack the windows."

"Perfect."

"Buckle up."

The next few minutes were awkwardly silent as they pulled out of the parking lot, but at least Holden could pretend to be focused on watching the road. When they reached their first stoplight, it got really bad. Nothing to do then but wait for the light to change. Maybe some music? She'd probably hate his playlist, though.

What's up? I'm Mustardseed and videogame soundtracks are my jam.

Thankfully, Seyah broke the quiet. "So, the party's at Cleaver's house, right?"

"Uh, right." Holden had overheard vague rumblings about it, but he hadn't been officially invited. Technically, since he was a member of the cast, the invitation to the cast party was kind of automatic, but no one had come up to him specifically and said, "So Holden, we gonna see you at the party?"

"You know how to get there?" asked Seyah. "It's across town. We can skip a bunch of lights if we take the back roads. I know the way."

"Okay, sounds good." It actually sounded great, because Holden didn't have a clue where Cleaver lived.

Seyah navigated while Holden drove, which gave them something to talk about other than the lingering boy smell in his car. Eventually they both started to relax a little, and the talk drifted away from "turn left here" to something closer to a real conversation. At first they focused on the play, the one thing they had in common. Seyah complained about the director, Mr. Solomon, and how he trilled his *r*'s whenever he gave her a line reading. Together they bitched about the fog machine that made everything smell like ass.

By the time the conversation had gotten around to Holden's legs, he was feeling pretty good.

"No! You didn't." Seyah covered her mouth in mock horror.

"Seriously," said Holden. "If I didn't shave them then the hair kept sticking out through the tights! It was gross. I'm telling you, it's not easy being the only guy fairy in the play."

"Can I see? C'mon, just a peek."

"I'm kind of driving."

"Oh, my God, that's the best story ever." Seyah laughed

and the sound made Holden feel like Oberon himself, a king for a day. Or at least a car ride.

"We all have our moments," he said, building up steam. "Andy Phillips scored the winning touchdown against the Tigers. I shaved my legs to play a fairy with no lines in the school play. I'd say we're in the same league of awesome."

"I think you just one-upped him. Also, Andy Phillips is a dick."

"Yeah, okay. But it's not as awesome as playing Titania. *Rocking* Titania. You rocked it."

Seyah cocked her head at him. "I *rocked* Shakespeare? Thanks."

"I'm serious. What's that line you say when you've been given the love potion? You know, after Bottom's been turned into a donkey."

"O, how I love thee! How I dote on thee!" she said, softly.

He watched her. Holden couldn't tell for sure in the dark, but Seyah might have been blushing.

"Better keep your eyes on the road, Holden."

"Huh? Oh yeah, I am." With both hands on the steering wheel and eyes front, he said, "Onstage you have to say that line to a guy in a donkey mask, and yet I totally believe it. You're amazing."

"Try acting opposite Brad Sanders. Believe me, the mask helps."

"Is that what you want to do when you get out of school? Act?"

Seyah didn't answer right away. "I don't know. I love performing, I really do, but it's a little selfish, isn't it? My mom's family's really conservative—they're Persian—and they definitely wouldn't approve. And my dad's a cop. He says the world needs, like, doctors and social workers and engineers."

"Your dad's a cop? That explains the bumper sticker."

Seyah gave him a dubious look.

"I saw it when we were checking out your engine," he added quickly.

"Yeah. Well, he's brutal when I bring guys home. Answers the door in his uniform."

This was followed by a soft lull in the conversation, but unlike the strained silence from earlier, this one felt natural. It was easy to enjoy the night, the drive together. They'd left the town behind them for a long stretch of twisting country road called Route 30. Holden knew that some kids liked to really open it up on these back roads, but he was in no hurry to get to the party. Seyah would meet up with her friends, and he'd be left loitering alone by the keg. The only boy fairy, the odd man out. No, his plan was to drop her off at the party and then make a quiet exit. Seyah's friends could take her home from there. Holden had just this one car ride with her and he wanted to make it last. Besides, as his buzzing phone kept reminding him, he had other places he was supposed to be tonight. Someone he needed to see.

A splinter of guilt twisted in his gut, but he might never get this chance again.

Holden took a deep breath. "You know, um, can I tell you something?"

"Sure."

"I'm not even really that into Shakespeare. This was my first play ever, and the only reason I got the part is because they needed bodies."

"That's not true."

"It is. Especially boys. They wanted at least one boy fairy and . . . Look, I gotta tell you, the whole reason I joined the play was—"

"Sorry, wait a sec." Seyah reached over and drew her finger along Holden's neck. Her touch made his hair tingle.

She held her finger up to the glow of the dashboard clock for him to see. Her fingertip was covered in glittery grease paint.

Seyah smiled. "Look! Fairy dust."

The clock read 9:31.

The glitter paint on her fingertip suddenly sparkled as it caught the light from an oncoming car.

Seyah screamed his name. Holden jerked the wheel, but it was too late. They hit the truck head on.

• • •

Holden's neck hurt, but at least he could turn his head. In the dream he'd been paralyzed.

He pulled himself up to a sitting position and waited for the head rush to pass. Water was dripping somewhere nearby. *Plink . . . plink.* He must be in a hospital, though he didn't know how he'd gotten there. But he did remember someone screaming his name. And dreams. Terrible dreams.

He was sitting on a bed—no, not a bed, because it felt like hard plastic and there weren't any pillows or sheets. It was more like a slab. What kind of hospital put its patients on a slab? He felt a jolt of panic, and worried for a moment that he'd woken up in a morgue. There were always stories about people who got accidentally buried, or woke up in a crematorium . . .

He'd never been in a morgue, but he'd seen them in movies and it only took a quick glance around to reassure him that this wasn't any such thing. For one, there weren't any of those big drawers that they kept the cadavers in. This room was plain white and pretty much bare, lit by a row of panels in the ceiling. Most of those lights were burnt out except for the one that kept flickering off and on. As far as he could tell, his slab was the only one.

Autopsy table, maybe?

With a shiver, he scooted off the table as fast as he could. It wasn't until he stood up that he realized someone had dressed him in a plain red jumpsuit and a pair of weird slipper-sneakers. What kind of hospital dressed its patients in jumpsuits? When he rubbed his chin he discovered that he was freshly shaved.

"Hello?" he called, but no one answered. The only door in the room was round, like a hatch, with one of those wheel handles you'd see on a submarine. Not that Holden had ever been on a submarine.

But again, movies.

Cautiously, Holden tried turning the wheel. A ridiculous image popped into his head of the hatch opening and water

14

spilling into the room, as if that hatch was the only thing between him and an entire ocean. But the handle wouldn't budge.

"Hello? Anyone there?" He knocked, but no one answered. Maybe he was in intensive care. Maybe this was some kind of sterile room. Holden did a thorough check of his body, but he couldn't find any injuries—not even a bruise. He seemed perfectly healthy except for the dull ache in his neck. And as for the room being sterile, he soon discovered the source of the dripping noise. In one corner was a rust-colored stain where the ceiling tile had bulged and started to split. Brownish water dripped from the center of the stain into a nasty-looking puddle. A pipe in the ceiling must be leaking, or maybe there'd been a flood in a room above this one, wherever it was. A small vent high up in the wall blew in stale air, and the floor was covered in greasy scuff marks and smudges, like someone had been dragging furniture across the tiles. But the slab was the only thing in the room.

A greasy floor, a leaky ceiling, and flickering lights. If this was a hospital, then Holden was damn sure going to complain to someone. If it wasn't . . . well, he wasn't ready to go there. Not yet.

He decided to try the door one more time, putting all of his skinny weight into it, but the handle still wouldn't move for him. He knocked; he pounded and shouted and even asked nicely. No one answered. No one came.

Eventually he stopped pacing, gave up banging on the door, sat down on the slab, and waited. Someone had gone through all the trouble to put him here, and that meant they had to come sooner or later. Right?

While he waited, he tried to piece together what he could remember. His memories were hazy and filled with crazy dreams, the kind where you wake up only to realize that you're still sleeping. But he remembered driving in his car after the performance, his phone buzzing in his pocket.

And he remembered fairy dust.

"Seyah!" Holden pounded on the door harder this time, until he'd scraped his knuckles raw. "Hello? Anyone! Please, just tell me if my friend is all right! I think she was with me when I was brought here. C'mon! Open the goddamn door!"

As if in answer, the door began to shake. A soft vibration at first, tickling his fingers. Then Holden was thrown off his feet as the whole room shook so violently it felt like it was tipping. The echo of twisting metal rang out from somewhere nearby, followed by an explosion, as Holden clasped his hands over his head as protection. The world was about to end.

Finally, the shaking stopped and the room righted itself. Holden looked up, terrified to stand in case an aftershock hit and knocked him back down again. Then the flickering light went out completely and the room became pitch dark.

Was it an earthquake? Holden didn't even know where he was, and now he began to wonder if anyone else did, either. He pictured whatever was outside that door in ruins, hallways buried in rubble, and here he was trapped in a locked room. In the dark. Alone.

The drip of the leaking ceiling had gotten worse.

Plink plink plink plink.

His room had sprung a few more leaks.

As Holden sat there, listening to the dripping water and his own breathing and trying not to hyperventilate in the claustrophobic dark, his eyes slowly began to adjust. The room wasn't entirely lightless after all. There was a red sliver of light that hadn't been there before, near where the door must be. Cautiously, he groped forward through the dark on his hands and knees. As he crawled, his knees and palms got wet, and drops of icy water sprinkled his head and back.

Plink plink plink plink.

The red light was coming from narrow gaps where the door hatch met the wall. He explored with his hands and felt a new bulge that ran from ceiling to floor. The quake must have damaged the wall as well, and those cracks were the seams where the door had pulled away. There was no telling how structurally sound this place was now, and if there was an aftershock, the whole place might collapse on top of him. It could be only a matter of time.

Holden studied the door. It was difficult to see much,

but that light was definitely coming from whatever was on the other side. Holden put his eye up to the crack and saw an empty hallway. A track of red emergency lights ran along the floor.

As Holden felt around the edges of the door, he found that it had nearly torn free from one of its hinges. He could probably force it open now. Then again, that sturdy metal door might be the only thing keeping the wall from collapsing entirely. But what other choice did he have? Wait for another quake to bring the whole place down? Sit in the dark and slowly starve to death, hoping for rescue that might never come?

He tried the door's wheel handle again. It didn't move at first, but when Holden put a little muscle behind it, something gave way with a crack and the wheel spun free. The bolt had snapped clean off; that hatch would never lock again. The only problem was that, because of the warped wall and the torn hinge, the hatch wouldn't open more than a foot or so, and Holden didn't want to force it any more than he had to.

For the first time in his life, Holden was thankful for being on the scrawny side. As it was, he barely squeezed through the narrow opening and managed to leave only a little skin behind.

He found himself in a narrow hallway with low ceilings. The emergency lights were spaced a good distance apart, so it was hard to make out details in either direction. As for which direction he should go, if he'd had a coin, he would've flipped it.

He chose to go right. The walls and ceilings were the same plastic as his room, but here the floors were made of interlocking metal grates. When Holden crouched low, he could see cables and pipes running underneath. The lack of any windows gave him the feeling of being underground. Was this some kind of bunker? Or just the basement level of a hospital? He hoped it was the latter, even though the more he explored, the less and less likely that possibility seemed. The walls looked stable, though he did come across a section

17

of hallway where several of the ceiling tiles had collapsed, exposing more cables above. He picked his way past the debris, careful not to touch the dangling cables in case there was a live current, and continued on.

He passed other hatches, but they were all locked. After knocking on the first few, he gave up.

"Hello? Anybody there?" The lonely sound of his voice echoing back at him started to creep him out almost as much as the dark. He didn't have to worry about his imagination running away with him—reality was strange enough. What the hell was this place and why was he the only person around?

Holden felt an immediate urge to see the sun. To feel the wind on his face and look up at the open sky. He was suffocating and the only way to breathe was to get *out*.

He quickened his pace, stumbling now and then in the dark but not caring. Up ahead was an intersection where the hallway continued to wind to the left, but next to the track of emergency lights was a ladder that disappeared into a shaft in the ceiling. If he was underground, then up was the way to go.

Holden had never liked close spaces, but the fear of being buried alive in this place sent him up the ladder, one hand over the other, into a shaft narrow enough that he could touch every wall with an outstretched hand.

The air down below had been stale and musty, but he hadn't climbed far before that began to change. It was cooler up there, despite the cramped space, and the air tasted different— humid. The red emergency lights ended and Holden found himself climbing toward an open hatch lit by a greenish blue glow. The light shimmered.

As Holden lifted himself through, he could hardly believe what he saw. The shaft deposited him onto a platform overlooking an enclosed lake, half the length of a football field. The water was at least fifteen or twenty feet deep, as far as he could tell, and lit by rows of yellow lights along the bottom, like a swimming pool at night. Those that hadn't burnt out cast the chamber in a wavy, shimmering glow. A narrow metal bridge spanned the lake from his platform to a door barely visible on the far end. The ladder continued upward until it reached a web of catwalks that crisscrossed the high ceiling, most of which was hidden in shadow. One section of the catwalk above had collapsed near the far end of the lake, where the wreckage of metal bars and cables stuck out of the water like the mast of a sunken ship.

It was no wonder Holden's room leaked. It was directly beneath a giant reservoir. Forget being crushed by the earthquake—Holden had been in as much danger of drowning.

The ladder up didn't look very promising, and since part of the catwalk had already collapsed, Holden tested the bridge instead. It seemed sturdy enough. He stepped gingerly out onto it. The artificial lake stretched on either side of him, its glimmering lights deep below him.

Gone was the sense of claustrophobia, but it was replaced by a new fear. The high ceilings that disappeared into darkness and the immense lake all around him left Holden feeling exposed. His soft-soled shoes barely made a sound against the metal bridge, but in this silent cavern even the smallest noise felt like it was disturbing the dark. He kept eyeing the water, nervously, but the surface stayed still, smooth as glass.

Holden tried his best to ignore the sound of his own footsteps as he made his way across the bridge. The wreckage from the fallen catwalk lay between him and the distant doorway, but it didn't look impassible. He might have to do some climbing, but he could manage that.

Holden was halfway across the bridge when a new sound echoed through the chamber—a scraping noise, like metal dragging across metal. Holden stopped and turned, squinting against the dark. The water was still, undisturbed. The bridge behind him was empty.

The sound came again, only this time louder and less like scraping and more like . . . scuttling. Holden didn't dare to breathe as he finally looked up. The distant ceiling was mostly hidden in deep shadow, but movement caught his eye. Something was crawling along the catwalk.

No. Crawling *under* the catwalk, suspended there. The shimmering light from the reservoir caught a cluster of red, prism-like eyes.

"Holden!"

A face appeared from behind the wreckage. Brown skin, big eyes, but no crown of leaves in her hair anymore.

Seyah.

"Holden!" she shouted. "Run!"

He did. Not back the way he'd come, but toward her. To Seyah. He could hear metal legs still clicking overhead as the thing kept pace with him. Seyah wasn't watching Holden anymore. She was staring with horror at the creature stalking him from above. Holden didn't look up. He pumped his legs as fast as he could. He ran for Seyah.

He nearly slammed into the wrecked catwalk as he skidded to a halt and started to climb.

"Hurry, hurry!" Seyah shouted as Holden hoisted himself over the twisted fallen railings that formed a barricade between him and the doorway.

His foot slipped, and he caught himself on a piece of jagged metal, tearing open his palm. He tumbled to the floor, but he'd cleared the wreckage.

Then Seyah was by his side, pulling him along with her as they stumbled together toward the doorway. Something large dropped from above and the platform shook as it landed behind Holden and Seyah. Metal legs. Many metal legs scraping along the walkway.

They reached the doorway and Holden tried to push Seyah through first, but she tripped and fell, taking Holden down with her.

Out of the corner of his eye Holden caught a glimpse of the large, spiderlike thing looming over them. Red eyes burned bright.

Then a shape appeared in the doorway, and rough, calloused fingers grabbed Holden and Seyah. Holden's arm was nearly yanked out of its socket as a hand dragged him through the open doorway.

The door slammed shut behind them.

It was like waking from a familiar nightmare. Holden pulled himself to a sitting position, clutching his bleeding hand to his chest. Seyah was already getting to her feet. The person who'd slammed the door shut behind them was a stocky woman in a red jumpsuit. She spun the handle wheel until it locked in place, then turned to face Holden. She had a wide forehead and a heavy brow that hung over small eyes. A lumpy, too-broad nose dominated her long face and prominent hairy jaw.

Holden had seen that face before. "You . . ."

"Come," the woman said. Her voice was raspy, her words deliberate. "Doors do not stop them."

Seyah helped Holden to his feet. "Let's go."

"Wait, I remember her," he said, still staring at the woman. "What the hell's going on? What was that thing back there?"

Seyah took Holden by the arm. "I know you're freaking out, but we have to go now. We'll explain later, I promise."

Holden wanted to grab the woman and shout at her, to make her tell him what was going on. What had she said to him in his dream? *We'll wake you when it's all over.* Because it hadn't been a dream. He was awake, but it wasn't over. Far from it.

"Holden!" said Seyah again. He could hear the panic in her voice.

"Okay," he said. "Which way?"

"Follow me," said the woman, and the three of them ran. They hadn't gone far before Holden heard the sound of the door being torn from its hinges, followed by a loud clang.

"Faster!" called the woman, and the three of them sprinted through a maze of tunnels that flashed by in twists and turns. The distance between them grew, and Holden was falling behind. Then he took what he immediately realized was a wrong turn. He heard Seyah calling his name, and, just as he started to turn around, he spotted a partially open hatchway.

Unlike the other rooms, this one wasn't lit by the emergency lighting. A bright natural light shone in there. Perhaps it was a way out.

Holden opened the hatch the rest of the way. Both

Seyah and the woman caught up with him. They'd doubled back.

"No!" said the woman. "Not there!"

But it was too late. The door was open and Holden was looking at what she didn't want him to see. The light inside the room came from a floor-to-ceiling window, and on the other side . . .

At first, he couldn't understand what he was looking at. Of course he'd seen the white swirling clouds, the green-and-brown continents and blue oceans before. Everyone knew what the planet Earth looked like from space. But that was in photos and movies.

Holden held on to the hatch door for support. He felt the woman's arms grab him around the middle as he sagged forward and retched. As his stomach convulsed and struggled to bring up food that wasn't there, the woman held him and gently rubbed his back.

They weren't in some bunker deep under the earth. They were floating above it.

• • •

"You did better than me," said the woman.

"I puked everywhere," said Holden. "What did you do?"

"Tried to break the glass," she said. "Seyah, water?"

Wordlessly, Seyah dug a plain plastic bottle out of the backpack she was wearing. All three of them were dressed in identical jumpsuits. Seyah was the only one carrying a backpack.

The woman wet a small cloth from her pocket and handed it to Holden.

"Thanks." He did the best he could to clean himself off.

After Holden's freak-out at the observatory window, they'd crawled up a small service shaft and hidden in an empty storage room. It had taken a few minutes to catch their breath, but the woman had finally declared that they were safe for the time being.

"Who are you?" Holden asked the woman.

"Umta." Again, there was that slow, careful quality to her speech, like someone who was uncomfortable in a foreign language, but Holden didn't catch any trace of an accent.

"I'm Holden."

The woman, Umta, nodded.

"But you knew that."

"Seyah told me your name," said Umta.

Holden looked to Seyah for confirmation, but she turned away and didn't say anything. She'd been acting strange ever since they'd stopped running. At first she'd seemed so relieved to see him, just as he'd been to find her alive. They'd run from that creature, whatever it was, arm in arm. She'd probably saved his life. But after the immediate threat was over, Seyah had retreated into herself. She kept glancing over her shoulder, arms folded protectively across her chest, always on the lookout for danger.

"What's happening?" asked Holden. "Am I . . . are we really . . ."

"Above the Earth," said Umta. "High above." The note of awe in Umta's voice was unmistakable. Despite all that he'd seen, Holden wasn't sure he could accept any of it. But he wanted to hear what else Umta had to say. Then he'd decide whether he'd started hallucinating or not.

"How did we get here?"

"What do you remember?" said Umta.

Holden thought for a moment. There were a lot of images in his head, but they were all mixed up. Fragmented. "I think I remember you. I was on a table and these . . . spider things were hurting me. Like that one back there."

Umta shook her head. "Not that. Not yet. Before the dreams."

Holden looked at Seyah. "Uh, I was driving, with Seyah. We were in my car."

"Then there were lights," said Seyah, staring at Holden. Hurt in those eyes. Anger, even. "A truck's headlights right in front of us."

And there was the unspoken accusation: *the truck you drove us into.*

23

"Yeah." Holden looked away, remembering Seyah's face as she'd wiped a bit of glitter paint off his neck. Just before she'd screamed. "There was a car wreck."

"Nothing more?" asked Umta.

"No," said Holden. "Did we end up in a hospital or . . ."

Holden's words trailed off as Seyah burst out laughing. "Don't you get it? We hit a truck head on. No one survives something like that."

"Seyah," said Umta. "He needs time."

"We fucking died, Holden!"

Holden waited for the punch line. When none came, he got mad. "What the hell, Seyah? Are you trying to tell me that *this* is heaven?"

Umta held up her hand. "This is not easy."

But Seyah got to her feet. "I'm going to keep a lookout. I've heard this all before." She stomped over to the service shaft and planted herself at the edge, her back to Holden and Umta.

"She woke up before you," said Umta. "But it is still hard for her."

"What is? Accepting that we're dead?"

"Not dead now." Umta poked him in the chest. "You are alive now, you are breathing now. But do you remember dying *then*?"

Holden remembered the headlights. He remembered Seyah screaming his name. That was it. But she was right about one thing—he didn't understand how anyone could survive a crash like that. "I'm not sure what I remember."

Umta grunted. "Maybe that is good for you."

Holden put his head in his hands. If he'd had anything left in his stomach to puke up, he would have done it. This wasn't happening.

"Where is this place?" asked Holden. "I mean, I know it seems like we're in space or whatever, but this place is huge! The US doesn't have anything like that. No one does. And what was that thing back there that chased us? Some kind of alien?"

Umta shook her head. "No. They are machines. They

24

call themselves *caretakers.*"

"They spoke to you?"

"Not with words."

"Then how?"

"Data . . . images. Ideas. I knew they wanted to help. To care for me."

It was hard not to stare at Umta. It wasn't only that she was truly ugly. There was something so odd about her, the way she spoke, the way she moved. He wondered if she had some kind of medical condition, but that wasn't the kind of thing you could ask a person.

"I thought I dreamed about you, but that wasn't a dream, was it?"

"No."

"And those metal spiders in my dream were the same thing. Caretakers, right?"

"They were trying to care for you," said Umta. "Not like the other one."

"But they were torturing me."

"They . . . they do not understand pain like we do."

"Look, if these things want to help us so badly, why was that one chasing us back there?"

Umta sat on her heels and picked at her toes. Holden hadn't even realized that she wasn't wearing shoes. She kept at one thick, yellow toenail as she spoke. "Yesterday more caretakers came. Like that one. Two tribes fighting over territory. The new tribe won."

"Let me guess," said Holden. "These new *caretakers* don't want to care for us at all."

"No." Umta wouldn't look at him. "I do not think so."

"Christ."

Seyah spoke up from her seat near the service shaft. "It doesn't matter. We need to get out of here. Get back home." She had been listening after all.

"There is a way," explained Umta. "I can take you there."

"What, like a shuttle?" asked Holden. "I don't think any of us can pilot a space shuttle."

"She says it's an elevator," said Seyah.

Holden got to his feet. "Excuse me? We're in space."

"Orbital elevator," said Umta. "From the station to the planet."

"Why haven't I heard of this?" said Holden. "If someone built something like that, I think that would make the news."

"Hey, we're supposed to be dead, right?" said Seyah, glaring at him. "So who knows?"

There was a time when Holden would have done anything to be around Seyah Jackson. Even dress up like a boy fairy to be close to her, just so she'd look at him. But the way she looked at him now was devastating. And Holden understood. After all, he'd been the one driving the car. A car that she should have never been in. If Holden hadn't lied about not having jumper cables. If he hadn't driven to that party instead of . . .

There was so much Seyah didn't even know. She had real reasons to be angry with him. To hate him.

He took a deep breath. "Okay, so you know where this elevator is?"

"Umta was taking me there," said Seyah. She paused. "I told her we needed to find you first."

"No more time to talk," said Umta. "We are close now."

At that moment another tremor shook the station. Not strong enough to knock them off their feet, but unmistakable.

Umta stepped up to take the lead. "The station was damaged in the fighting. It is not safe."

Holden whispered under his breath, "No shit."

This time Umta avoided the main hallways and led them through a twisting maze of narrow service tunnels. Too narrow, they hoped, for the caretakers. It occurred to Holden that though it felt abandoned now, this space station had definitely been built with people in mind. The architecture was familiar, and giant metal spiders didn't need ladders to get around. The station had been built by human beings to be used by human beings.

The tremors were getting more and more frequent. It felt like the station was coming apart around them. There wasn't any time to waste.

Holden was running on adrenaline; maybe it was only the flood of chemicals in his system that kept him from falling down and screaming, even as his brain could barely accept what was happening to him. Or maybe it was Seyah. Whatever was going on, she was here with him. He felt responsible for that. For her.

Umta led them to a lightless, horizontal air shaft, and Seyah handed each of them a glow stick from her backpack.

"Where did you find these?" Holden asked.

"Umta knew where a supply locker was. I grabbed these lights, some water bottles, and some things that look like protein bars. Umta swears they taste like tree bark. There were extra clothes too but I couldn't fit everything into the pack."

Holden grimaced. If they lived long enough to need to worry about a change of clothes, he'd be thrilled.

They crawled into the air shaft single file, on their hands and knees. Umta took the lead several yards ahead of them.

He tried to talk to Seyah as they went. "How long have you been here? I mean, awake."

"Keep your voice down," she said.

"I am. I'm just trying to figure stuff out."

"Things were blurry at first."

"Did you see any of those caretaker things?"

Seyah shook her head. "Just the dreams. The spider dreams. When I woke up I was locked inside a bare room."

"And when was that?"

Seyah hesitated before answering. "Yesterday."

"And that's when all this fighting started?"

"Yeah, I think so. Umta showed up and told me all that stuff about the caretakers, and how we were in danger. She made me hide while she went off to make sure the elevator was still working. Then she showed up again and told me that it was time to go and here we are."

"Listen." Holden lowered his voice to barely a whisper. "I don't want to sound like a dick, but how does she know so much about this place? Are you sure we can trust her? We barely even know her."

Seyah stopped and looked over her shoulder at him.

"Holden, I barely know *you*."

She was right, of course. Holden had been watching Seyah Jackson from afar for years. She was beautiful, popular. She'd been the kind of student that people talked about. He'd developed a crush early on, and he really felt like he'd gotten to know her. Maybe it was the way people think they know celebrities, but he felt a connection. To her he was just some quiet guy with a bit part in her play.

She sighed. "Look, we're going to lose Umta if we don't speed up."

"Okay."

Seyah started crawling again. "And stop staring at my butt."

Holden was right behind her, face burning as he kept his eyes glued to the floor.

By the time they reached the right air vent, Holden's legs and arms were cramped from all the crawling, and he dreamed of nothing more than simply standing up. According to Umta, on the other side of that vent was the door to the orbital elevator. Which was good, because the entire time they'd been crawling around in the air shafts they hadn't felt so much as a breeze. It looked like the air they had now was all they had—and who knew how long it would last. Plus, it was getting colder. Holden's teeth were chattering, and he breathed on his fingers to keep them from going numb. It made sense, he supposed. If the caretakers wanted to kill them then the easiest way would be to knock out the life support. Machines don't need to breathe.

"Let's hurry," said Seyah. "I can see my own breath."

Umta leaned into the vent, blocking their way into the room beyond. "Here, if we push together—"

Umta didn't finish her sentence though, because at that moment a young man's round face appeared on the other side of the vent, scaring the hell out of them.

"There you are!" he said.

Umta grunted at him. "Thomas!"

Holden looked at Seyah and mouthed, "Thomas?"

She shook her head. Seyah had no idea who he was

either.

With Thomas helping, the three of them climbed out of the vent and stretched the knots and kinks out of their sore arms and legs.

"Thomas," said Umta. "Why are you still here?"

Thomas, who didn't seem any older than Holden and might have been a year or two younger, even, blushed. "I . . . I wanted to make sure you were okay."

Umta cocked her head at him, visibly frustrated.

"Okay, and I'm scared of heights," he said. "Seriously, that elevator, it's just freaky."

The room they were in had a closed hatchway on one wall and several benches where waiting passengers could gaze out a window at the planet below. A pair of sliding doors led to the elevator itself, but they were closed. Holden peered out the window and saw a massive tower of cable and girders outside. The sun had set on this hemisphere and the miles-long stalk of the orbital elevator reached down through the stratosphere and into the dark cloud cover far below. He couldn't blame Thomas. The view gave him vertigo too. They were supposed to ride that thing all the way down to the ground?

"Umta," said Seyah. "You didn't tell me there were other people on the station."

"There should not be anymore," said Umta. Then, turning to the boy, she said, "Thomas, come with us—"

Umta was cut off by a loud clang. Then the lock on the hatchway behind them gave a sudden pop and the door swung open slowly to reveal a spindly legged shadow just beyond.

Holden's first impression of a giant metal spider had been close, but not exact. As it stepped through the hatchway and into the lighted room, the caretaker reminded Holden more of an upright sarcophagus balanced on eight metal legs. The multifaceted, insect-like eyes were arranged in a cluster so that it could watch all directions at once. But at that moment it was only watching them.

"Run!" shouted Umta, and they ran for the elevator doors. Umta grabbed Holden by the arm, pressing his hand up against a glassy display panel on the wall.

"What are you doing?" he shouted.

"Has to be human," was all she said, and in response to Holden's touch, the doors slid open with a soft whoosh. But then the caretaker flicked one of its legs and a metal cord, like a whip, shot toward them. Holden shoved Seyah forward, knocking them both to the ground, and the cord snapped above their heads. But it caught Thomas.

He screamed as the caretaker yanked him backward, lifting him by his feet like a fish on a line.

It dangled him there in front of its many eyes. They glowed red as they studied him.

Umta screamed at the thing. The sound was something between a wail and a roar.

In answer, several of the caretaker's legs reared up at once, and Holden could only watch in horror as it began to take Thomas apart. It was methodical, efficient. This wasn't a murder; it was a dissection.

Umta wailed in despair. Holden tugged on her arm. He knew she was in shock, but it was too late to save Thomas, and they couldn't stay there. He just kept thinking, *It will be done with Thomas soon . . .*

With Seyah's help, he dragged Umta into the elevator. The doors began to slide closed behind them, but it was like they were moving in slow motion, an aperture gradually closing on the horror of what was happening in the next room.

For a fraction of a second, before the doors closed entirely, the caretaker paused its bloody work and looked directly at Holden. It let out a terrible sound, something between the squealing of a car braking too fast and the screeching of some wild, wounded animal. Then the doors sealed shut and everything went quiet.

There were no controls that they could see, only seats ringing the car. Holden and Seyah threw themselves into the two seats farthest from the door. Umta slumped to the floor and stayed right where she was.

Any second now those doors would open back up again. Any second now they would be cut into pieces.

"Go, go, go!" Seyah was saying under her breath. She

was shaking.

The car jerked as they started their descent.

The elevator moved so slowly as to feel ponderous. But then it probably had to. Holden remembered reading something about the g-forces astronauts experienced upon reentry. Any faster and this space elevator would deliver a can of soup to the ground below. So they were in for a long ride back to Earth, but at least they were moving away from the station.

"Is everyone all right?" he asked. Seyah barely nodded. Umta didn't bother to answer at all; she just put her head down on her knees. After that no one said much of anything. Like the station, the elevator had obviously been built with humans in mind. Holden found a small bathroom closet, but little else. Seyah produced a bottle of water from her pack and split it with Holden. When they offered some to Umta, she said nothing.

The stars gleamed bright past the stratosphere, and Holden and Seyah sat by the window as they watched the station gradually disappear. In the far distance, they could see a second elevator tethered to another low-orbit station. It looked so close, but in reality it had to be thousands of miles away.

After a while the silence became too much for Holden. "Umta, who was Thomas?"

Seyah shot him a look, but Holden ignored it.

"Umta?"

Umta lay in a ball on the floor, absently picking at her hair. She answered without looking up. "Too dangerous to lead all of you through the station at the same time. He was supposed to go down without me. I told him to."

"Down where?" said Holden. "Where are we escaping to?"

Umta sighed. "I hope someplace better."

Lying there on the floor, Umta looked almost primitive. As Holden really examined her features, he found they weren't simply unattractive, the too-heavy forehead and the wide, flat nose. At first glance he'd wondered if Umta suffered from some kind of deformity, but now Holden didn't think that was the case. Because he remembered what she'd said to him when she pressed his hand to the elevator's control panel. She wouldn't or couldn't activate the elevator herself.

It has to be human, she'd said.

"Umta," said Holden. "When *were* you taken?"

She looked up at him now, her eyes red from crying. Such tired eyes. "Long before you, I think. Long, long ago."

Then she lay her head back down in the crook of her arm and closed her eyes. Soon she was asleep, and every now and then she whimpered as she dreamed.

Hours passed. Seyah was lost in her own thoughts and Umta slept, so Holden found himself staring down at his own feet. That's when he realized his shoes were spattered with rust-colored dots. Thomas's blood. When he closed his eyes that was all he saw. That, and the red eyes of the caretaker looking back at him.

If it hadn't been Thomas, it would have been one of us. That could've been Seyah's blood on his shoes.

"What if those things came to Earth while we were unconscious after the car crash?" Holden spoke quietly so as not to wake Umta. "We could've been out for months. What if in that time, there was an alien invasion by those caretakers? Maybe they invaded and starting using these space elevators to snatch up people like us for their crazy alien experiments."

Seyah shook her head. "So you think we're gonna get down there and find an alien flag over the White House?"

"I'm just trying to make some sense of all this. But we'll see when we get there, won't we?"

"Yeah, I suppose so." She turned back to the window "Nothing to do now but wait, I guess."

"We could wake Umta," said Holden. "She has to know more about all this."

"I don't know. I think she's more or less in the same boat we are. I think she woke up on that station just like we did, only she was alone until we came along. That kid, Thomas. Maybe others. She's weird, you know? And not so great at communicating, if you hadn't noticed."

Holden thought about telling her what Umta had said, about needing a *human* hand to operate the elevator doors. Who was she, really? He considered shaking her awake, demanding answers. But maybe Seyah was right. Maybe Umta was just as scared and lost as they were. She certainly seemed to be in shock.

"I gotta take a leak," he said.

He stepped into the little closet and was reminded at once of an airplane restroom. The only thing lacking was a mirror and that chemical smell. He pissed in the little commode, but though he found what looked like a button to flush, he couldn't bring himself to push it. He had an irrational image of getting sucked out through the toilet. They were still so high up.

He scraped the blood off his shoes as best he could. There wasn't a faucet, but there was a disinfectant dispenser that was out of disinfectant. It was stupid after all he'd been through, but he found himself wishing for a mirror so he could straighten himself up. Despite everything, he couldn't let it go that that was Seyah Jackson in the next room.

When he returned, Seyah was standing at the window, staring down at something.

"What's wrong?" he asked.

"I don't think . . . Just come look."

Holden joined her at the window, and he caught his reflection in the glass. He looked like hell. "What is it?"

"We've broken through the clouds."

Holden cupped has hands over his eyes and pressed his face against the glass.

"I can't see anything. It's all black."

"That's what I mean," said Seyah. "If that's really Earth, then where are all the lights?"

Holden looked again. She was right. The earth was blue and green in the daytime, but at night he should have been able to see the light of cities and towns. Humankind's footprint on the planet was most visible at night. But tonight the world below them was lightless.

"What do you think it means?" she asked.

"Massive blackout?"

"All of North America? Assuming that is North America."

Holden didn't have an answer for that. He hadn't really had an answer for anything since waking up.

Without being able to see the ground, they could only assume they were getting close to landing when the elevator began to slow. They strapped themselves back into their seats as a bell chimed. Umta woke and sat up. The elevator came to an abrupt stop.

"Guess we're here," said Seyah.

Holden unbuckled himself and peered out the window. It was hard to make out details in the dark. "Looks like trees, maybe?"

Umta rummaged through Seyah's backpack until she found the glow sticks. She handed them each one. "These still have a few hours of light left in them. I will go first." Umta stood at the elevator door for a moment, staring at the glass panel.

Seyah gave Holden a confused glance, but he knew what was expected. Wordlessly, he placed his hand on the panel, and the doors slid open.

By the light of their glow sticks they found they'd arrived at a waiting room much like the one they'd escaped from above. A thick layer of dust coated everything.

"What do you think?" asked Seyah.

"Hold on." Holden tried lifting one of the plastic benches, but they were all bolted to the ground. He spotted a few extra chairs stacked in a corner and picked one up. "Grab one of these, will you?"

"Why?"

"I don't want our elevator going back up and bringing down those caretakers." He jammed the chair in as best he could so that the elevator doors couldn't close all the way. With Seyah's help, he stacked up several more. Umta watched but said nothing.

"That should do it," he said.

"You think a few chairs will stop them?" said Seyah.

"If the doors won't shut, then the elevator won't move, right?"

Seyah shook her head, but didn't have any better suggestions, so they looked for a way out. They found a hatchway that wasn't locked, and the wheel turned easily.

Beyond the hatch it was nighttime in a wilderness. There was a patch of pink barely visible in what they assumed was the east, so dawn wasn't far off. Trees crowded around them and they could hear the loud droning of insects, the calls of early morning birds.

"Weird place to build a space elevator," said Holden.

Umta took a glow stick from Seyah and shined it on the ground in front of her, poking her fingers around in the muddy grass. "Tracks. This way."

"Wait," said Seyah. "Where are we going?"

"To find the others," answered Umta.

"Others?" said Holden, but Umta was already marching off through the forest. He and Seyah had to rush to catch up.

It was hard going. In the dark, Holden kept discovering hidden roots by tripping over them, and Umta stayed twenty or so yards ahead of them, but they never lost sight of her glow stick. As they marched through the trees, the blue-black sky above lightened into a misty new day. Through the dense leaves they caught glimpses of mountains in the morning fog. As the trees thinned out up ahead, Umta stopped and waited for them to catch up.

She had stepped through a break in the trees and now stood there staring in awe. When Holden and Seyah caught up with her, Seyah let out a little gasp and Holden instinctively reached for her hand. She didn't pull it away. The mountain range they'd glimpsed before wasn't a mountain range at all. In the distance stood a line of towering skyscrapers. But the buildings were little more than husks of metal and shattered glass. Birds nested in the broken-out windows. A stream meandered down the center of it all where a street should have been. They'd reached the outskirts of a ruined city that had been swallowed up by the forest itself.

Standing there a few yards away was a group of teens all

dressed in the same red jumpsuits that Holden, Seyah, and Umta wore. Some were busy constructing a makeshift camp, while some were still staring up in wonder at the overgrown city. Others turned to watch Holden, Seyah, and Umta approach.

One of them, an Asian girl, ran forward. "Let me guess. You don't know anything, and you don't have any food."

SERIAL
BOX

Join the Plot

We hope you enjoyed the first episode of ReMade!

ReMade premiers September 14, 2016, with episodes releasing every week until the first season wraps.

To get it, download our app from the Apple app store, subscribe at www.serialbox.com/serials/remade, or buy episodes from your favorite eBook retailer.

New episodes are released each Wednesday in both text and audio forms. Subscribers automatically receive episodes delivered to their devices.

ReMade Writing Team

Matthew Cody hails from St. Louis and holds a Master's Degree in Theater from the University of Alabama with a focus on Shakespeare. He is a graduate of the Clarion Writers Workshop and currently resides New York City with his family. His published works include the award winning *Powerless* and *The Supers of Noble's Green* series, the Robin Hood re-imaging *Will in Scarlet*, and his current series *The Secrets of the Pied Piper*. Matthew-Cody.com. @Matthew_Cody.

Kiersten White is the NYT bestselling author of the *Paranormalcy* trilogy, the *Mind Games* series, *Illusions of Fate*, *The Chaos of Stars*, *In the Shadows* with artist Jim Di Bartolo, and the upcoming historical reimagining, *And I Darken*. She has one tall husband and three small children and lives near the ocean, where her life is perfectly normal. She also gives the world's most awkward hugs. kierstenwhite.com. @KierstenWhite.

E. C. Myers was assembled in the U.S. from Korean and German parts and raised by a single mother and a public library in Yonkers, New York. He garnered a degree in Visual Arts from Columbia University which he completely neglects to use in his current life as a freelance writer and editor. A graduate of Clarion West, his stories have been published in *Kaleidoscope: Diverse YA Science*

Fiction and Fantasy Stories, Andromeda Spaceways Inflight Magazine, and *Space and Time* magazine. His novel *Fair Coin* won the Andre Norton Award for Young Adult Science Fiction and Fantasy. ECMyers. net. @ECMyers.

Andrea Phillips is a transmedia writer, game designer and author. She is on the writing team for season 2 of the urban fantasy serial Bookburners as well as ReMade. Her debut novel is *Revision*, an SF thriller about a wiki where your edits come true. She has also worked on iOS fitness games *Zombies, Run!* and *The Walk; The Maester's Path* for HBO's Game of Thrones; human rights game *America 2049*; and the independent commercial ARG *Perplex City*. She also writes an ongoing column about video games called "Metagames" for *Strange Horizons.* Her nonfiction book *A Creator's Guide to Transmedia Storytelling* is used to teach digital storytelling at universities around the world. AndreaPhillips.com. @Andrhia.

Carrie Harris was born in Chicago but if you ask her, she'll say she's from Ohio. Her interests include English Literature, brains, and hot geek boys. She has held a string of very incongruous jobs but in between autopsies and studying mad cows, she wrote for various tabletop roleplaying games and textbook companies. These days she writes books for teens, tweens, and adults while also being the Marketing Director for Evil Hat Productions. Her published works include *Bad Taste*

in Boys and *Demon Derby*. CarrieHarris-Books.com. @CarrHarr.

Gwenda Bond writes for children and young adults. Her books include *Lois Lane: Fallout, Girl on a Wire,* and *Girl in the Shadows,* as well as the graphic novel *Girl Over Paris* with Kate Leth and Ming Doyle. She holds an MFA in writing from the Vermont College of Fine Arts and has written for *Publishers Weekly,* the *Los Angeles Times,* and the *Washington Post* amongst others. She currently resides in a hundred-year-old house in Lexington, Kentucky with her husband and their menagerie. GwendaBond.com. @Gwenda.